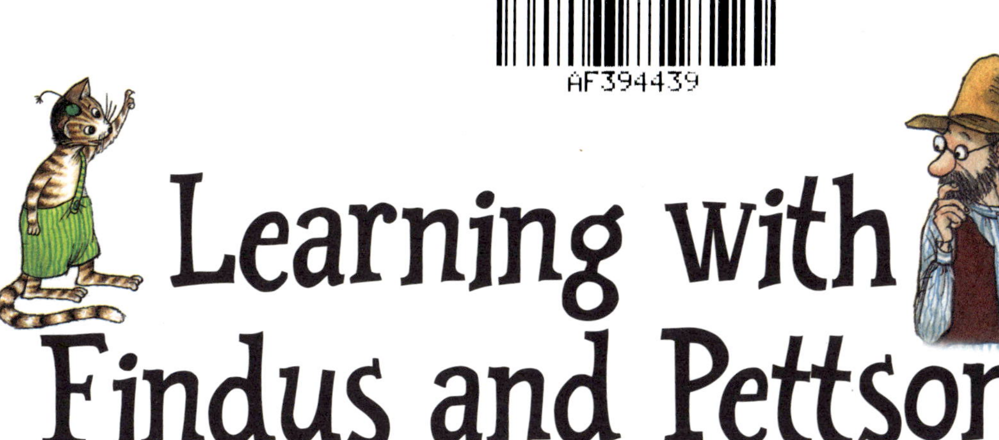

Learning with Findus and Pettson

Numbers and Shapes

Hawthorn Press

Findus's Shadow

Findus jumps around so much his shadow can't keep up. Can you help by drawing a line between Findus and the right shadow?

Jigsaw Time!

It is nice and cosy in the kitchen, but
what's happened to the picture?
Can you put the pieces in the right place?

1.

2.

3.

How will the Muckle get Home?

The little muckle is lost and can't find the way home.
Which of the three paths is the right one?

Vegetable Count 

It's spring and Findus is busy with his vegetable patch.
How many plants are there in each row?

Muckle Colour Sudoku

The clever muckles have made their own sudoku. Can you fill all the boxes with the right colour? Each colour may appear only once in each row, column and box.

Paint by Numbers

Who is hiding in the grid? Follow the number guide to colour in the boxes and you will see.

1.    2.    3.   4.

Find Your Way in the Garden

Pettson and Findus are in the garden. They have found a list of directions. Start at the X and follow the directions to see what they are looking for.

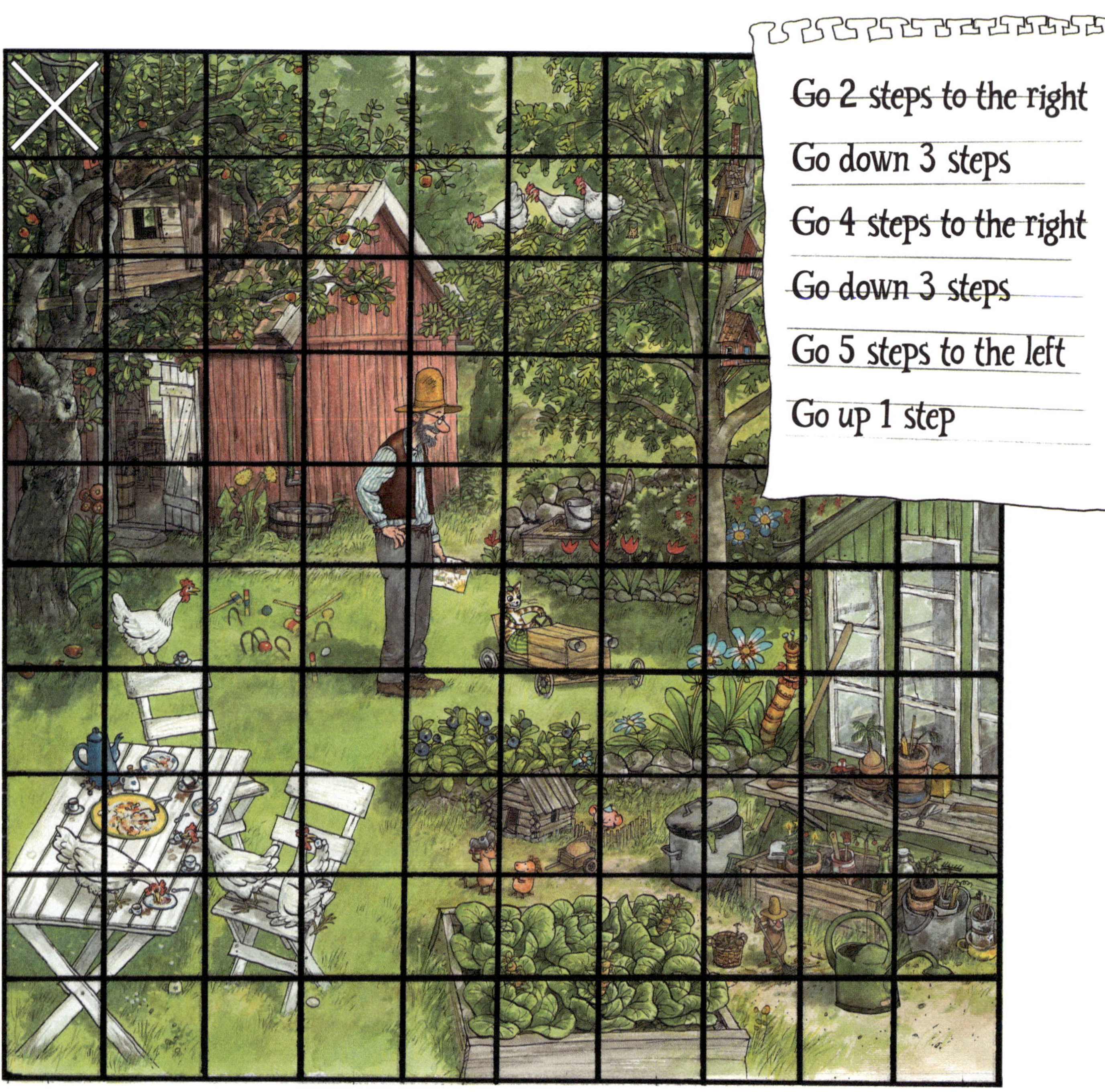

I CAN SEE: ___________________________

Loads of Apples

Findus and the hens compete to see who can load the most apples into their wheelbarrows. But who wins? Count the apples and write the number in each wheelbarrow.

Missing Piece

Sitting like this with Pettson is one of Findus's favourite things. But there is a piece of the picture missing. Which of the 3 pieces below is the right one?

1.

2.

3.

Fill the Trolleys

Each muckle wants 4 pears on their trolley.
Draw more pears so that everyone gets enough.

Dot to Dot

This looks strange. What is hiding in the picture?
Join the dots from 1 to 38 to find out!

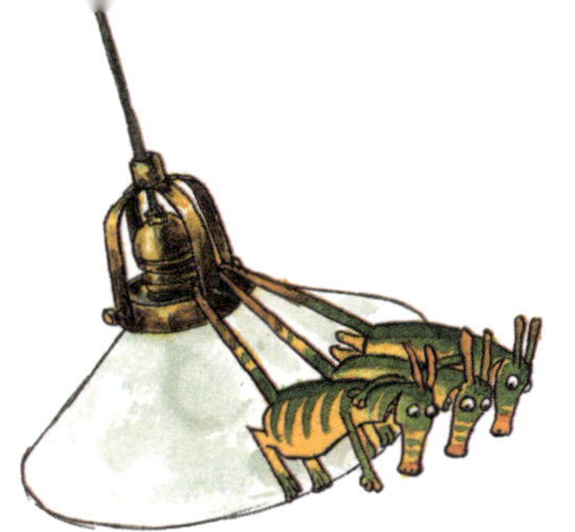

Paint by Numbers

Pettson's clothes have lost their colours!
Use the colour guide to paint them back.

1.  **2.**  **3.**  **4.**

Secret Muckle Code 

The muckles have invented a secret way to count.
Can you solve the additions below?

 = 1    = 4   = 7

= 2   = 5   = 8

= 3   = 6   = 9

 **+**  **=**

+ **=**

Number Maze

The hen is looking for her eggs that
Pettson collected this morning. But she can
only step on number 5 or higher.
Draw a line through the numbers to show
her how to get to the basket of eggs.

6	8	1	0	9	7	0	3	8	3
3	5	5	4	6	3	7	9	2	7
5	2	7	9	3	6	6	4	4	9
1	0	4	6	7	3	2	5	7	5
9	7	2	3	5	2	7	1	9	4
8	4	9	5	6	1	3	2	6	3
9	6	8	7	3	8	5	7	8	6
3	9	6	8	9	7	3	5	3	8
2	2	3	4	8	2	1	4	2	6
7	6	1	7	1	6	8	7	1	3

Continue the Pattern

Findus has made some pretty patterns and is feeling very pleased with himself. Can you figure out the rule for each pattern and fill in the blanks?

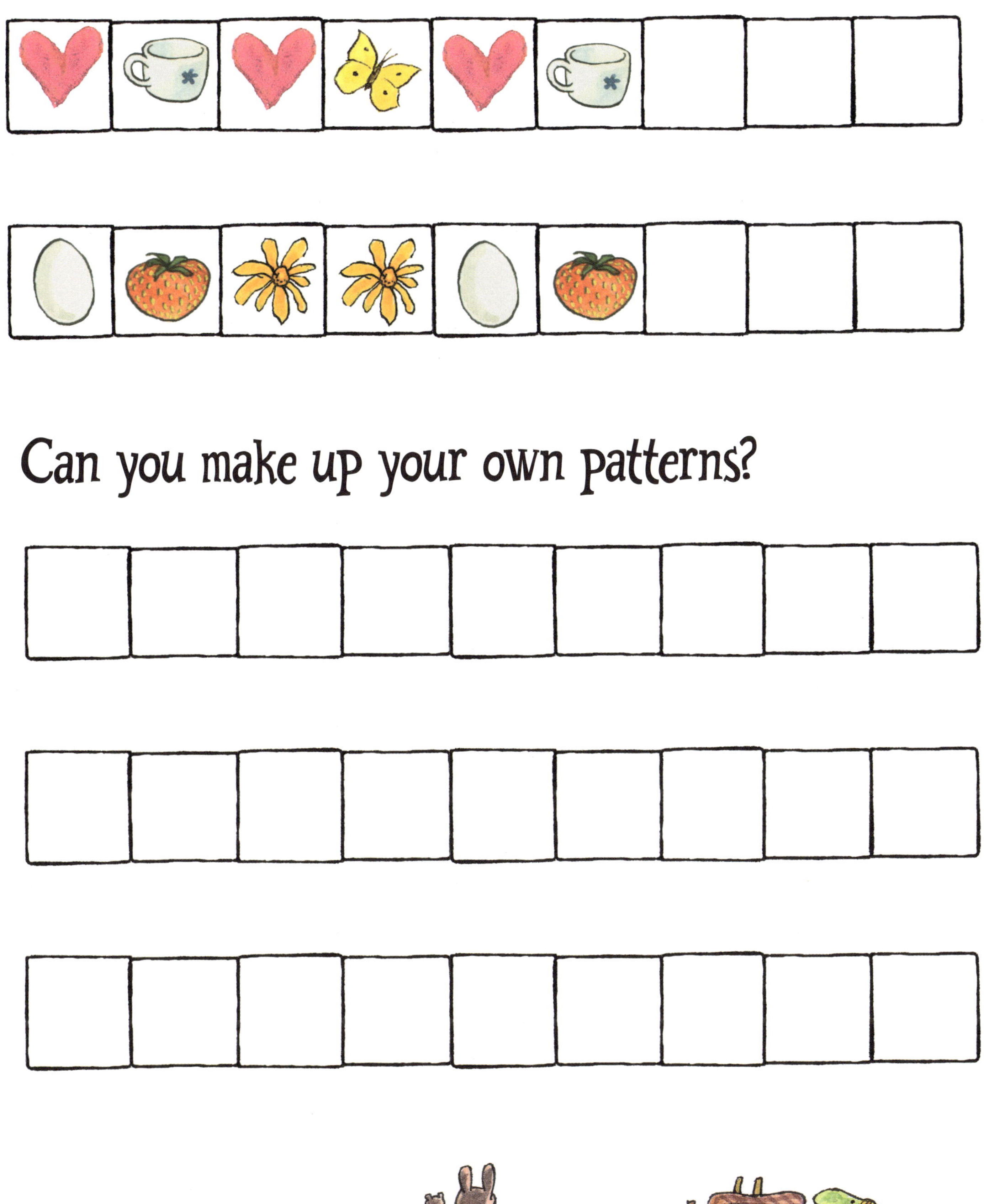

Can you make up your own patterns?

Lost Cockerel

The poor cockerel is lost in the garden.
Can you guide him through the maze
and back to the hens?

Count the Shapes

Pettson and Findus have made their own
cookie cutters, but they are all jumbled up!
Can you count how many there are of each shape?

Add and Subtract

One Findus is the same as one muckle, or one hen.
But how many hens, muckles and Finduses are
there in these sums? Can you solve these puzzles
and write in the correct number?

Which is the Longest?

Findus has dragged some stuff out of the shed.
He asks the muckles if they can tell which object is the
longest. Can you? Number the objects from 1 to 4
with 1 being the longest and 4 being the shortest.

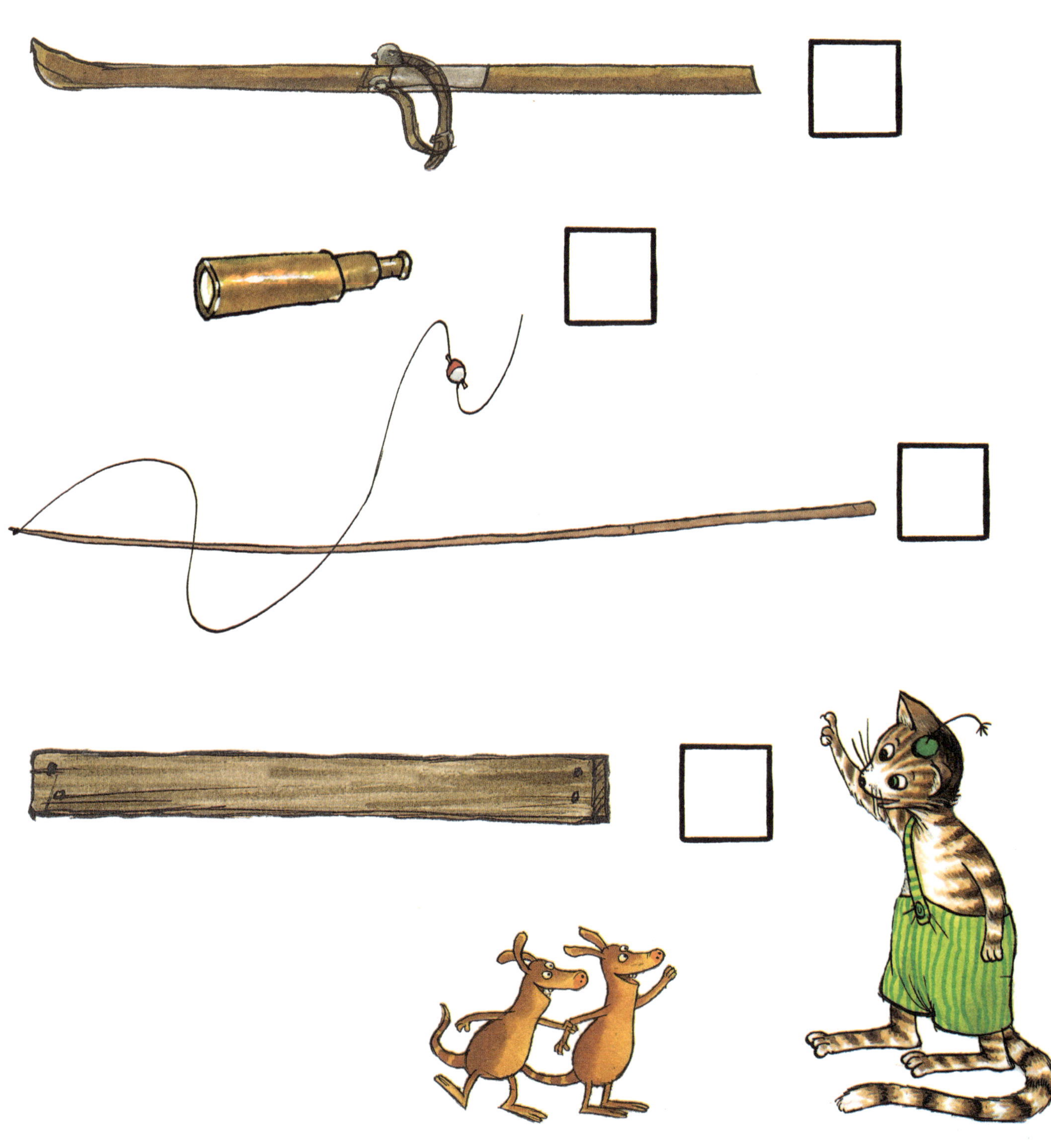

Muckle Count

Sometimes Findus seems to see muckles
everywhere he looks. But how many of each
kind of muckle are there actually?

Find the Pairs

Here are lots of objects, but one of them is lonely.
Find and circle the object that doesn't have a friend.

Colour

Oh no! It looks like Pettson and Findus are so busy making pancakes that they haven't noticed they have lost their colour. Can you colour them back in?

Secret Muckle Code

The muckles have been busy making some more puzzles.
Can you figure out the answers?

= 1	= 4	= 7
= 2	= 5	= 8
= 3	= 6	= 9

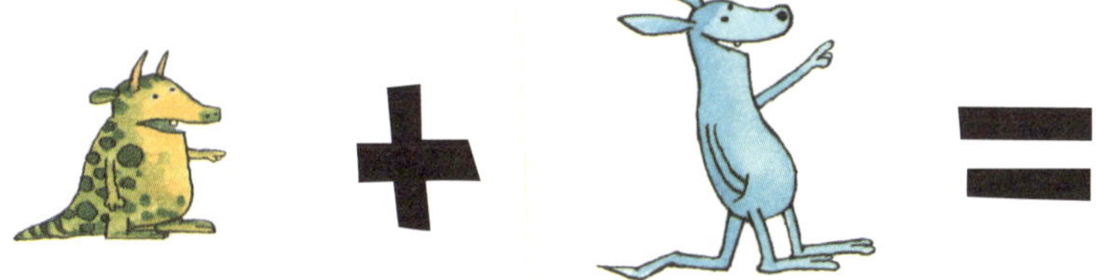

Muckle Colour Sudoku

The muckles have made another sudoku.
See if you can solve this one too.

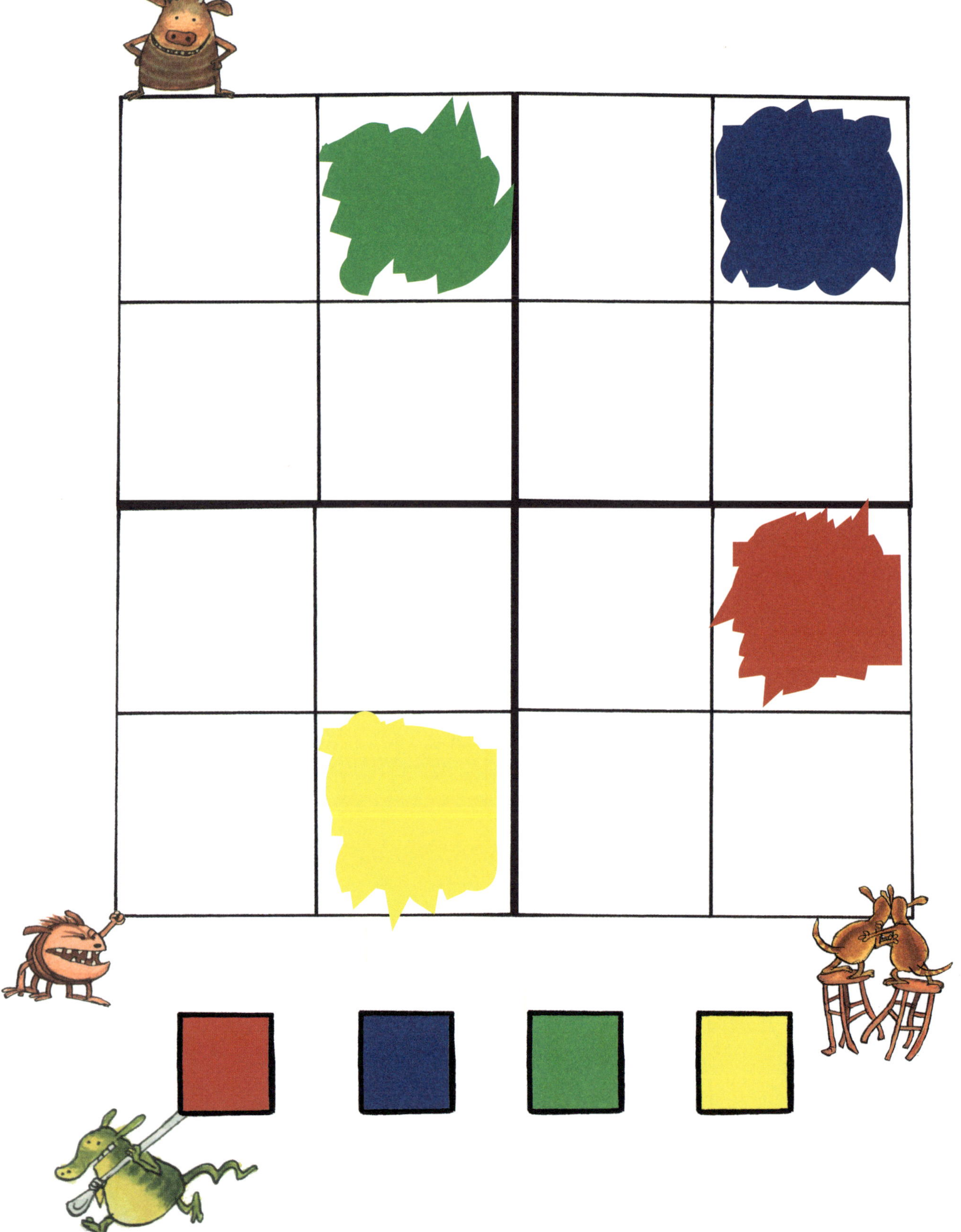

0 1 2 3 4 5 6 7 8 9 10
11 12 13 14 15 16 17 18
19 20 21 22 23 24 25
26 27 28 29 30 31 32
33 34 35 36 37 38 30
40 41 42 43 44 45 46
47 48 49 50 51 52 53
54 55 56 57 58 59 60
61 62 63 64 65 66 67
68 69 70 71 72 73 74
75 76 77 78 79 80 81 82
83 84 85 86 87 88 89 90
91 92 93 94 95 96 97 99

Answers

— 2 —
Findus's Shadow

Findus jumps around so much his shadow can't keep up. Can you help by drawing a line between Findus and the right shadow?

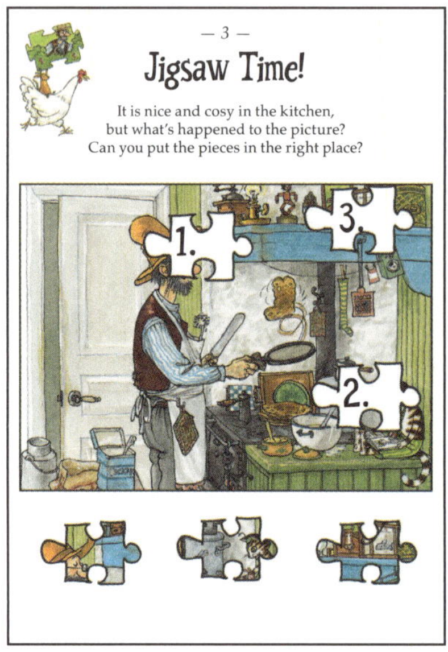

— 3 —
Jigsaw Time!

It is nice and cosy in the kitchen, but what's happened to the picture? Can you put the pieces in the right place?

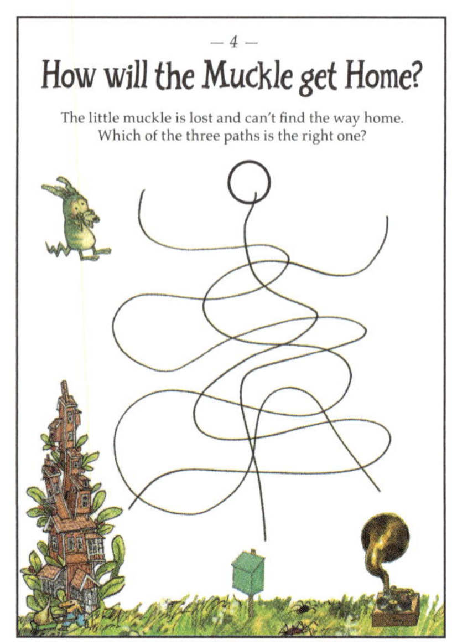

— 4 —
How will the Muckle get Home?

The little muckle is lost and can't find the way home. Which of the three paths is the right one?

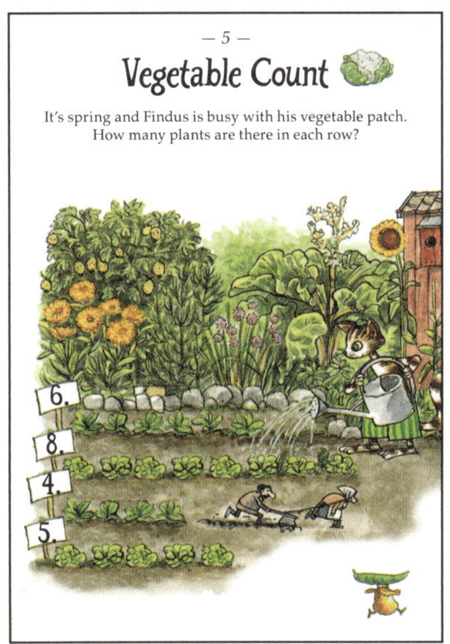

— 5 —
Vegetable Count

It's spring and Findus is busy with his vegetable patch. How many plants are there in each row?

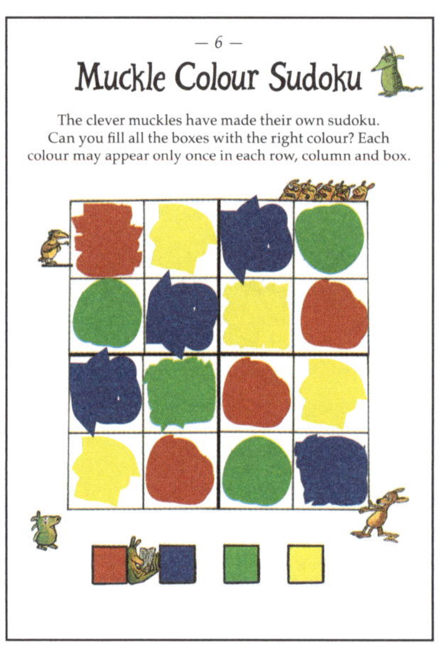

— 6 —
Muckle Colour Sudoku

The clever muckles have made their own sudoku. Can you fill all the boxes with the right colour? Each colour may appear only once in each row, column and box.

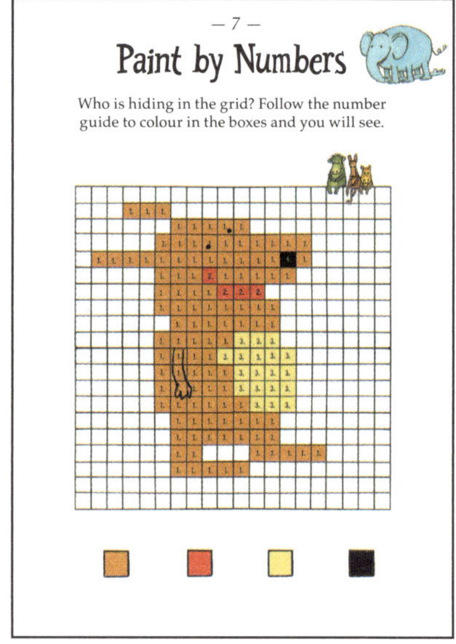

— 7 —
Paint by Numbers

Who is hiding in the grid? Follow the number guide to colour in the boxes and you will see.

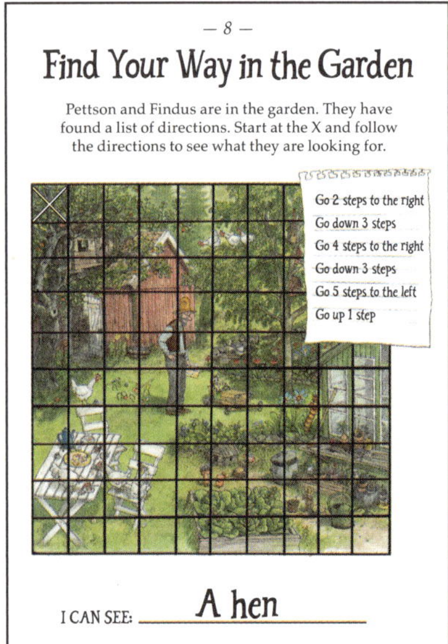

— 8 —
Find Your Way in the Garden

Pettson and Findus are in the garden. They have found a list of directions. Start at the X and follow the directions to see what they are looking for.

I CAN SEE: __A hen__

— 9 —
Loads of Apples

Findus and the hens compete to see who can load the most apples into their wheelbarrows. But who wins? Count the apples and write the number in each wheelbarrow.

— 10 —
Missing Piece

Sitting like this with Pettson is one of Findus's favourite things. But there is a piece of the picture missing. Which of the 3 pieces below is the right one?

Answers

— 11 —
Fill the Trolleys

Each muckle wants 4 pears on their trolley.
Draw more pears so that everyone gets enough.

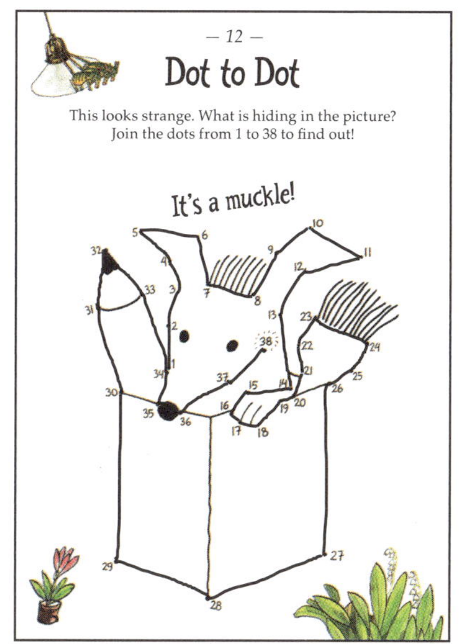

— 12 —
Dot to Dot

This looks strange. What is hiding in the picture?
Join the dots from 1 to 38 to find out!

It's a muckle!

— 13 —
Paint by Numbers

Pettson's clothes have lost their colours!
Use the colour guide to paint them back.

1.   2.   3.   4.

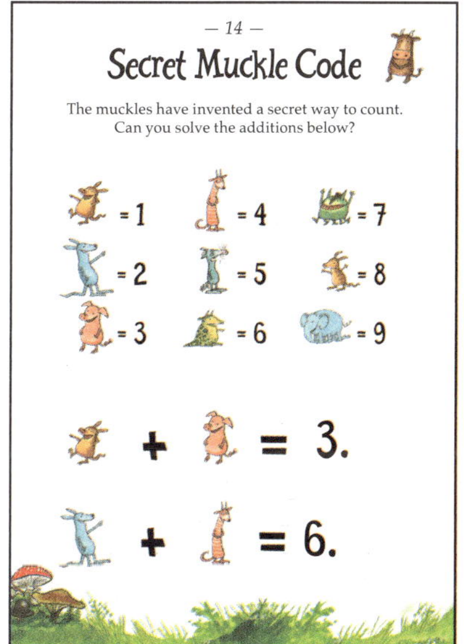

— 14 —
Secret Muckle Code

The muckles have invented a secret way to count.
Can you solve the additions below?

= 1   = 4   = 7
= 2   = 5   = 8
= 3   = 6   = 9

+ = 3.

+ = 6.

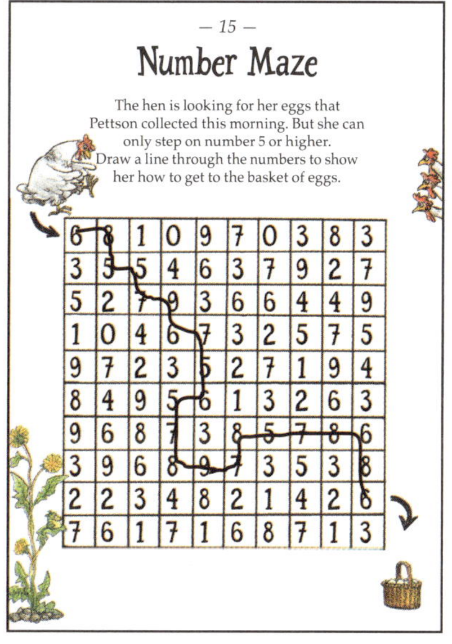

— 15 —
Number Maze

The hen is looking for her eggs that
Pettson collected this morning. But she can
only step on number 5 or higher.
Draw a line through the numbers to show
her how to get to the basket of eggs.

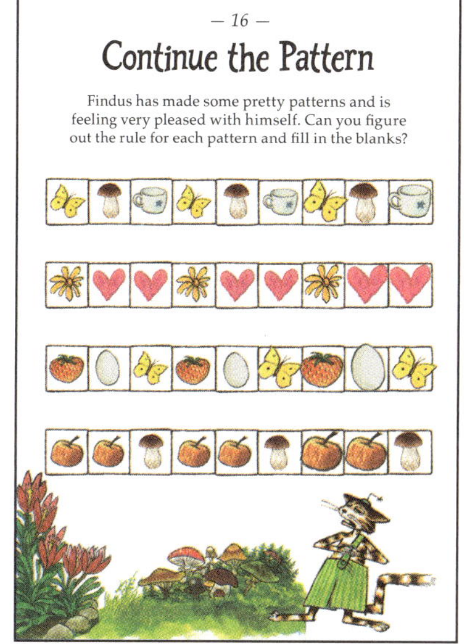

— 16 —
Continue the Pattern

Findus has made some pretty patterns and is
feeling very pleased with himself. Can you figure
out the rule for each pattern and fill in the blanks?

— 17 —

Can you make up your own patterns?

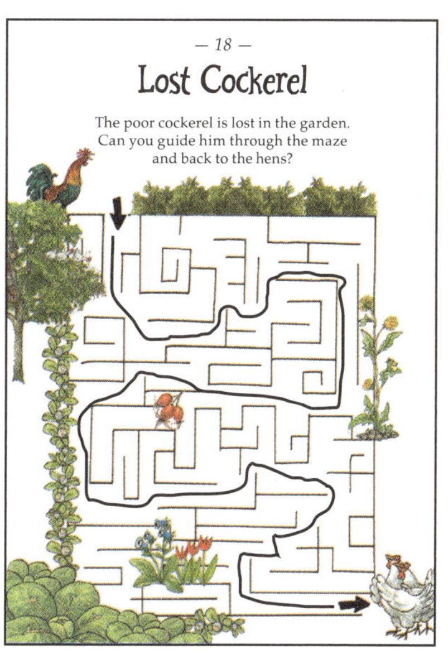

— 18 —
Lost Cockerel

The poor cockerel is lost in the garden.
Can you guide him through the maze
and back to the hens?

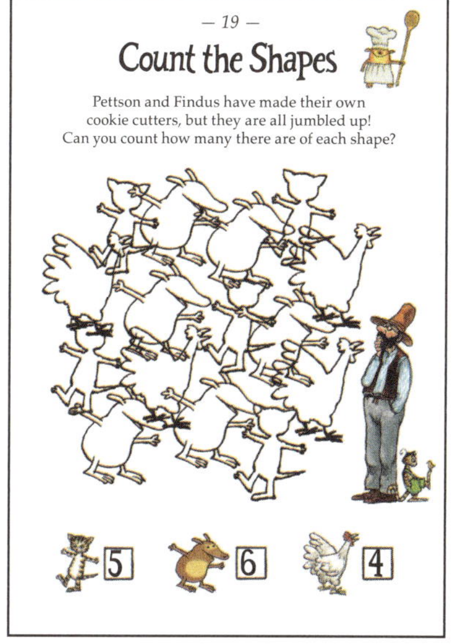

— 19 —
Count the Shapes

Pettson and Findus have made their own
cookie cutters, but they are all jumbled up!
Can you count how many there are of each shape?

5   6   4

Answers

— 20 —
Add and Subtract
One Findus is the same as one muckle, or one hen.
But how many hens, muckles and Finduses are
there in these sums? Can you solve these puzzles
and write in the correct number?
=5
=7

— 21 —
+ =3
+ =6
− =3

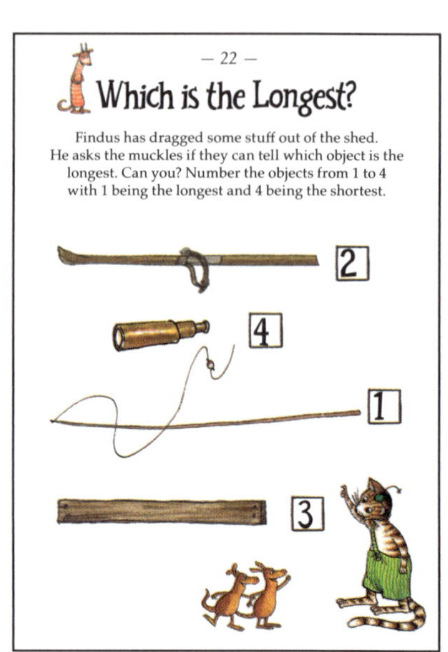
— 22 —
Which is the Longest?
Findus has dragged some stuff out of the shed.
He asks the muckles if they can tell which object is the
longest. Can you? Number the objects from 1 to 4
with 1 being the longest and 4 being the shortest.
2
4
1
3

— 23 —
Muckle Count
Sometimes Findus seems to see muckles
everywhere he looks. But how many of each
kind of muckle are there actually?
7 6 7

— 24 —
Find the Pairs
Here are lots of objects, but one of them is lonely.
Find and circle the object that doesn't have a friend.

— 25 —
Colour
Oh no! It looks like Pettson and Findus are so busy
making pancakes that they haven't noticed they have
lost their colour. Can you colour them back in?

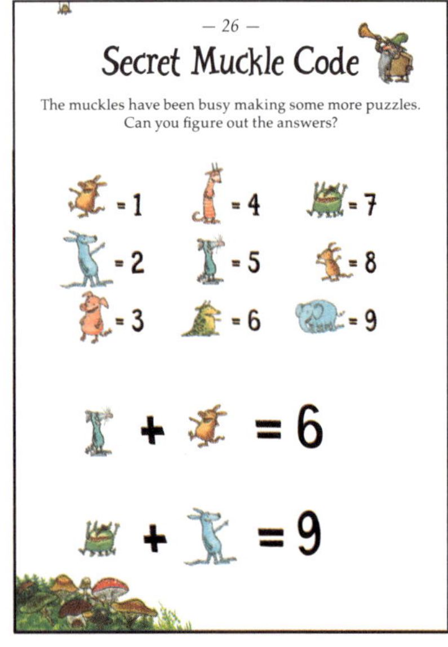
— 26 —
Secret Muckle Code
The muckles have been busy making some more puzzles.
Can you figure out the answers?
=1 =4 =7
=2 =5 =8
=3 =6 =9
+ = 6
+ = 9

— 27 —
+ =7
+ =8
− =8
− =1
− =4

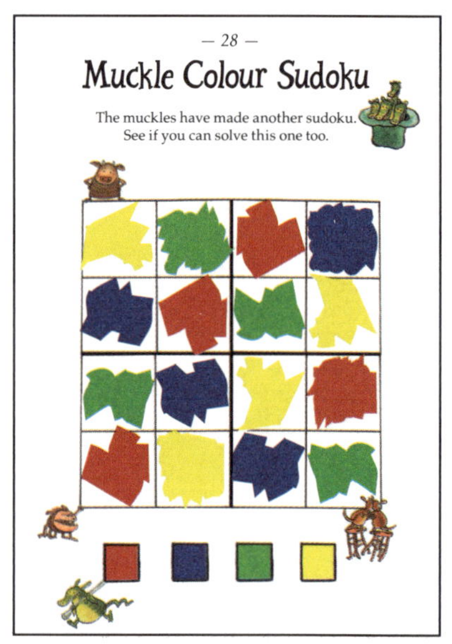
— 28 —
Muckle Colour Sudoku
The muckles have made another sudoku.
See if you can solve this one too.